rv

BEFORE CANADA:
FIRST NATIONS AND FIRST CONTACTS

Prehistory~1523

TITLE LIST

Before Canada: First Nations and First Contacts, Prehistory–1523

The Settlement of New France and Acadia, 1524–1701

Britain's Canada, 1613–1770

Conflicts, Changes, and Confederation, 1770–1867

From the Atlantic to the Pacific: Canadian Expansion, 1867–1909

A Nation Is Born: World War I and Independence, 1910–1929

Crisis at Home and Abroad:
The Great Depression, World War II, and Beyond, 1929–1959

Redefining Canada: A Developing Identity, 1960–1984

Canada's Changing Society, 1984–the Present

Canada's Modern-Day First Nations:
Nunavut and Evolving Relationships

BEFORE CANADA:
FIRST NATIONS AND FIRST CONTACTS

Prehistory~1523

BY
SHEILA NELSON

MASON CREST PUBLISHERS
PHILADELPHIA

Mason Crest Publishers Inc.
370 Reed Road
Broomall, Pennsylvania 19008
(866) MCP-BOOK (toll free)

First printing
1 2 3 4 5 6 7 8 9 10

Library of Congress Cataloging-in-Publication Data

Nelson, Sheila.
  Before Canada : First Nations and first contacts : prehistory–1523 / by Sheila Nelson.
     p. cm.
  Includes index.
  ISBN 1-4222-0001-9   ISBN 1-4222-0000-0 (series)
  1. Indians of North America—Canada—History—Juvenile literature. 2. Indians of North America—First contact with Europeans—Juvenile literature. 3. Canada—Antiquities—Juvenile literature. I. Title.
  E78.C2N45 2006
  971.01'1—dc22
                              2005002744

Produced by Harding House Publishing Service, Inc.
www.hardinghousepages.com
Interior design by MK Bassett-Harvey.
Cover design by Dianne Hodack.
Printed in the Hashemite Kingdom of Jordan.

CONTENTS

INTRODUCTION

by David Bercuson

Every country's history is distinct, and so is Canada's. Although Canada is often said to be a pale imitation of the United States, it has a unique history that has created a modern North American nation on its own path to democracy and social justice. This series explains how that happened.

Canada's history is rooted in its climate, its geography, and in its separate political development. Virtually all of Canada experiences long, dark, and very cold winters with copious amounts of snowfall. Canada also spans several distinct geographic regions, from the rugged western mountain ranges on the Pacific coast to the forested lowlands of the St. Lawrence River Valley and the Atlantic tidewater region.

Canada's regional divisions were complicated by the British conquest of New France at the end of the Seven Years' War in 1763. Although Britain defeated France, the French were far more numerous in Canada than the British. Britain was thus forced to recognize French Canadian rights to their own language, religion, and culture. That recognition is now enshrined in the Canadian Constitution. It has made Canada a democracy that values group rights alongside individual rights, with official French/English bilingualism as a key part of the Canadian character.

During the American Revolution, Canadians chose to stay British. After the Revolution, they provided refuge to tens of thousands of Americans who, for one reason or another, did not follow George Washington, Benjamin Franklin, or the other founders of the United States who broke with Britain.

Democracy in Canada under the British Crown evolved more slowly than it did in the United States. But in the early nineteenth century, slavery was outlawed in the

British Empire, and as a result, also in Canada. Thus Canada never experienced civil war or government-imposed racial segregation.

From these few, brief examples, it is clear that Canada's history differs considerably from that of the United States. And yet today, Canada is a true North American democracy in its own right. Canadians will profit from a better understanding of how their country was shaped—and Americans may learn much about their own country by studying the story of Canada.

Map of Canada

One

CANADA'S LAND: GEOLOGY AND GEOGRAPHY

Canada, the northernmost nation of North America, is the world's second-largest country. Its coasts touch three oceans: the Atlantic, Pacific, and Arctic. Because Canada is so large, its landscapes are vast and varied. From the rocky coasts of the Atlantic provinces to the rolling hills of the Prairies, the towering rain forests of British Columbia to the snow-swept tundra of the north, Canada is a country of variety and contrast. Canada is not only a land of diverse geographical regions; it's also a land of diverse peoples. Canada is a place where *tolerance* and *multiculturalism* thrive.

The Canada we know today, however, is a very recent arrival on the world scene. This nation has a rich past, and to fully understand the Canada of today, we must travel far back in time, for the history of Canada's land and people begins long before the country of Canada existed at all.

Tolerance means the acceptance of different views.

Multiculturalism is the existence of beliefs and customs from many cultures or civilizations.

*The **tectonic plates** are segments of the earth's crust. Their movement causes volcanic and earthquake activity around their margins.*

*A **fault** is a break in the rock layers of the earth's crust in response to stress.*

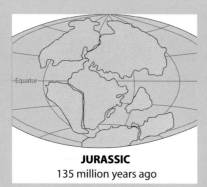

JURASSIC
135 million years ago

Map of Jurassic period

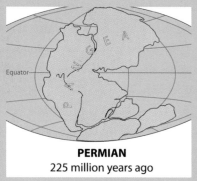

PERMIAN
225 million years ago

Map of Permian period

The Land Before Time

The land that makes up present-day Canada did not always look the way it appears on a modern map. If you could stand back and watch in fast-forward the movement of Earth's continents throughout history—millions of years going by in a matter of moments—you would see an amazing dance of land and water moving about the world. Continents, resting on their *tectonic plates*, would twist and shift, coming together, then moving apart again. Land would sink into the ocean. In another place, the ocean floor would rise up to become dry land. Great masses of earth would crash, collide, and slide back and forth until taking the shape of the continents as we know them today.

Earth's tectonic plates are approximately fifty miles (80.5 kilometers) thick and float on a bed of liquid rock. The plates shift about on this molten foundation, grinding against each other. Sometimes one plate slides beneath another, and huge mountain ranges wrinkle up along the *fault*. Where the plates move away from each other, volcanoes erupt, spewing the molten rock from deep within the earth. When this happens in the oceans, islands rise from the seas as the molten rock cools, hardens, and becomes new earth.

Hundreds of millions of years ago, the Earth's tectonic plates were huddled together in a single supercontinent called Pangaea. A little over 200 million years ago, Pangaea began to break apart, and the recognizable beginnings of the modern continents started moving away from each other.

Newfoundland's bedrock is visible beneath the thin soil.

11

The Geography of Canada

On the eastern side of what would become Canada, the island of Newfoundland formed when one piece of land broke off from the North American mainland and another broke from the area between southwestern Europe and northern Africa. Between these pieces, the ocean floor rose, joining the sections into a single island.

Volcanoes created new land forms.

12

Along the western side of the island, a small piece of the Earth's mantle—the deep semi-liquid rock below the crust—pushed up to join the mountains there. When the rocks hardened, they left a barren area where very little could grow. Millions of years later, this area located halfway down the west coast of Newfoundland, would become Gros Morne National Park.

On the continent's eastern mainland, the Appalachian Mountains rose, stretching from Newfoundland and Labrador in the north to Alabama in the southern United States. Today, eastern Canada consists of the Atlantic provinces—Newfoundland and Labrador (considered one province), Nova Scotia, Prince Edward Island, and New Brunswick. The mountains in these eastern provinces are now ancient and worn down. Along the coasts, waves crash against rocky cliffs or onto stretches of sandy beaches.

The Atlantic provinces are alike in many ways. They share an access to the ocean and an abundance of fish that has shaped their culture throughout history. Their summers are usually cool and their winters fairly mild. Each province has its own unique features, though.

Newfoundland, and its mainland counterpart Labrador, are rockier than the other provinces. Newfoundland's soil is thin, barely covering the underlying bedrock; bogs and ponds abound, and only inland, away from the winds blowing off the ocean,

Facts About Canada

Canada is 3,855,100 square miles (9,984,670 square kilometers), making it the second - largest country in the world (after Russia).

Canada has 125,567 miles (202,080 kilometers) of coastline, giving it the most coastline

do the trees grow to any great height. Along the coasts of Newfoundland's northern peninsula, the Atlantic's winds and salt spray stunt and twist the trees, which wrap around each other into knotted clumps called tuckamore. Newfoundland and Labrador is further north than the other Atlantic provinces, and the winters there are longer and harsher, especially in the northern regions.

The hills of Nova Scotia's Cape Breton Island are rich in minerals such as coal, gypsum, and salt. Along Nova Scotia's northwest side runs the Annapolis Valley, filled with some of the Atlantic provinces' most fertile soil.

Prince Edward Island is characterized by its rich red soil, perfect for growing potatoes. The island is tiny, low, and flat, with no real hills at all. The beaches are sandy and

Area of Canadian Provinces and Territories

Newfoundland and Labrador: 156,453 square miles (405,212 square kilometers)
Nova Scotia: 21,345 square miles (55,284 square kilometers)
Prince Edward Island: 2,185 square miles (5,660 square kilometers)
New Brunswick: 28,150 square miles (72,908 square kilometers)
Quebec: 595,391 square miles (1,542,056 square kilometers)
Ontario: 415,598 square miles (1,076,395 square kilometers)
Manitoba: 250,116 square miles (647,797 square kilometers)
Saskatchewan: 251,366 square miles (651,036 square kilometers)
Alberta: 255,541 square miles (661,848 square kilometers)
British Columbia: 364,764 square miles (944,735 square kilometers)
Yukon Territory: 186,272 square miles (482,443 square kilometers)
Northwest Territories: 519,734 square miles (1,346,106 square kilometers)
Nunavut: 808,185 square miles (2,093,190 square kilometers)

lined with red sandstone cliffs, which are constantly eroded by ocean waves.

New Brunswick lies the furthest inland of all the Atlantic provinces. Because of this, its forests grow taller and thicker, covering much of the province. The Bay of Fundy, along New Brunswick's southern shore, has the highest tides in the world. They rise and fall fifty feet (15.2 meters) in some places. The Reversing Falls are in St. John, New Brunswick, just before the St. John River empties into the Bay of Fundy; this phenomenon is caused by the high tides in the bay. At low tide, the river falls fourteen feet (4.3 meters) over rapids into the bay; the rising tides push the water back upstream along the St. John River, raising the water level above the rapids and causing the river to flow backward.

Just west of the Atlantic provinces are the central Canadian provinces of Ontario and Quebec. Two distinct areas—the St. Lawrence Lowlands and the Canadian Shield—characterize these provinces.

The St. Lawrence River flows from Lake Ontario northeast to the Atlantic Ocean, separating the main body of Quebec from the Gaspé Peninsula. Toward its eastern end, the river is so wide the opposite bank can barely be seen. The St. Lawrence has been extremely important in Canada's history and economy, since it offers a waterway leading to the Great Lakes and therefore provides access almost halfway across Canada.

Around the St. Lawrence River the land is low and flat, and the soil is very fertile. Long ago, trees covered most of the area; now, many of the forests have been cleared to make room for towns and cities. Its fertile land and mild climate made the St. Lawrence Lowlands, along with the Great

Map of Newfoundland, Labrador, Prince Edward Island, New Brunswick, and Nova Scotia

Lakes Lowlands, one of the most attractive areas of Canada for people throughout history, and, because of this, one of the most heavily populated.

The Canadian Shield is a huge area of ancient rock that covers over three million square miles (approximately 8 million square kilometers). It covers most of the provinces of Ontario and Quebec and extends into the bordering provinces as well. The Canadian Shield is sometimes called the Precambrian Shield, because it was created during the Precambrian Era, somewhere between 4.5 billion and 540 million years ago. This shield even predates the break up of Pangaea. Millions of years ago, the Canadian Shield was part of a mountain range. Over time, the mountaintops wore away, leaving

Nova Scotia's forests and streams

only their rocky bases. The bare rock that breaks through the thin soil of the Canadian Shield is some of the oldest visible rock in the world.

Minerals such as nickel, copper, silver, gold, and uranium abound in the Canadian Shield. The age of the rock, and the fact that for millions of years erosion has been grinding it down, means the minerals are quite close to the surface compared to other regions. In fact, the Canadian Shield is one of the most mineral-rich places on earth.

Thick forests, mostly made up of coniferous trees like spruce and fir, blanket huge parts of the shield. Although the soil is thin and acidic here, the trees grow thick and tall.

West of the Canadian Shield and the Great Lakes stretch the Prairie provinces of Manitoba, Saskatchewan, and Alberta. Millions of years ago, before the supercontinent Pangaea split apart, the land that is now the Prairie provinces lay at the bottom of the ocean. When the North American plate moved west, it pushed against the plate behind it, raising the ocean floor. As a result, the land of the southern Prairies is flat and fertile from the lakes of eastern Manitoba to the foothills of the Rockies in Alberta. The marine life that once lived in the area left the Prairies rich in fossil fuels like oil, gas, and coal.

In some areas of the Prairies, the land is completely flat; in others, rolling hills break up the horizon. In the flat, open areas of the south, few trees grow, and the sky looks huge.

North of the flat, southern grasslands, the land becomes forested, at first with leafy deciduous trees, then with thick forests of evergreens. In the most northern areas of the Prairie provinces the forests give way to the shrubby bushes of *tundra*.

*The **tundra** is a level, treeless plain located between the ice cap and the timber line of North America and Eurasia. Its subsoil is permanently frozen.*

The Yukon has long, bitter winters.

Canada's northern tundra

The Prairies experience more climate extremes than the rest of Canada. This is because they lie inland, away from the moderating effects of the ocean currents. They are also dry, with less than twelve inches (30 centimeters) of precipitation falling each year. The high Rocky Mountains to the west of the Prairies block most of the moisture that moves east off the Pacific Ocean. By the time the Pacific winds blow over the Rockies, they are dry. They gust across the open prairie land, evaporating moisture and drying the area still further.

West of the Rockies lie the province of British Columbia in the south and the Yukon Territory in the north. British Columbia and the Yukon Territory are part of the Cordillera region—a region of high, north–south running mountains. When the North American plate ran into the Pacific plate millions of years ago, it pushed its way over the Pacific plate, crumpling upward to form these towering western mountains.

British Columbia has two main mountain ranges: the Coast Mountains closest to the ocean, and the Rocky Mountains further to the east. These, as well as smaller mountain ranges, continue north into Yukon Territory. Between the mountain ranges is a wide, high valley, filled with open plains and forests. Many of the great western rivers spring from this area, winding their way back and forth between the mountain peaks before flowing into the Pacific.

Along the southern coast of British Columbia, temperatures are mild and rainfall is plentiful. The Coast Mountains block most of the moisture from moving east, and the clouds usually wring themselves out before blowing over the mountains. To the north, the temperatures are colder, the land next to the mountains more heavily forested with coniferous trees. In the Yukon Territory, winters are long and cold, without much precipitation, and summers are short and cool.

The fish from the oceans and rivers and the abundance of trees, especially in the northern regions, have attracted people to Canada's west coast for thousands of years. Furthermore, the mountains of the Cordillera contain vast amounts of minerals such as iron, lead, zinc, copper, nickel, silver, and gold. These natural resources have also drawn people to the region.

The vast northern areas of Canada—the Northwest Territories and Nunavut—are barren and snow swept for much of the year.

Nunavut's cold, barren land

19

*The **tree line** refers to the invisible boundary around the north pole, the south pole, and mountaintops, beyond which the climate is too cold to support tree growth.*

Most of the area lies north of the *tree line*, and much of it is north of the Arctic Circle as well. Instead of trees, grasses and small bushes cover the region. There are many islands, some of them covered with snow and ice year round.

Since the region is so far north, winter days are very short. In the middle of winter the sun rises for only a few hours. North of the Arctic Circle the sun does not rise at all in the dead of winter, while during the summer, the sunlight hours stretch on for most of the day, and the far north has several days of twenty-four-hour sunlight.

The Northern Lights

The Canadian North is one of the best places in the world for viewing the Aurora Borealis, or Northern Lights. The interaction of energized particles from the sun with the earth's atmosphere causes these dancing, colorful swirls of light. As these energized particles, or ions, fly past the earth, some are caught by earth's magnetic field and pulled down into the atmosphere. When these ions contact the atmospheric gases, they begin to glow. Earth's magnetic field is strongest at the poles, so it is at these places that the most ions get trapped and the auroras result. The Aurora Borealis's southern counterpart is the Aurora Australis, or Southern Lights.

The Northern Lights

Geographically, Canada is truly a land of variety and widely differing kinds of beauty. The processes that created these lands began billions of years before people ever arrived on the soil. Then, just tens of thousands of years ago (practically the blink of an eye in geological time), Canada began to change again. Human beings were arriving for the first time.

21

The frozen northern route to North America

Two
THE FIRST PEOPLE MIGRATE INTO NORTH AMERICA

Long ago, when snow and ice gripped the land, the people who hunted the mammoths began following the herds east across a wide, flat land that had not always been there. The people did not know the land had not always been there; they simply followed the herds of mammoths as they had done for generations.

Slowly, with their babies and all their belongings strapped on their backs, the people traveled further and further east. They used animal hides and bones to make tents, clothing, and tools. They were a strong people, used to surviving in a cold, harsh climate.

Glaciation is the process of becoming covered with ice.

This map shows the land bridge that once connected the continents of Asia and North America.

Scientists argue about when the first human beings crossed over from Asia into North America. Most agree that migrating people probably came across the Bering Land Bridge, a piece of land that connected Siberia to what is now Alaska. During the last Ice Age, heavy *glaciation* caused sea levels to fall, exposing more land and connecting Asia and North America, which had been separated by the impassable ocean. The most recent exposure of the Bering Land Bridge probably occurred from about 10,000 to 115,000 years ago. Few archaeologists agree on the exact time in this hundred-thousand-year period when humans began to arrive in North America, but most do agree that by fifteen to twenty thousand years ago, people had begun crossing the bridge.

The earliest travelers to North America would have worn thick furs.

The Inuit, like North America's first inhabitants, faced a harsh climate.

Beringia

Early travelers on the Bering Land Bridge needed to be a strong and determined people, since life in Beringia was far from easy. The glaciers lay further to the east, but winter temperatures still dropped far below freezing. Snow rarely fell, so tundra grasses were available to nourish the mammoths, muskoxen, bison, and antelopes, but no large trees grew to provide wood or sheltering windbreaks for humans.

Thousands of years ago, when the first people traveled across the Bering Land Bridge—sometimes called Beringia—huge glaciers covered almost all of Canada and reached south into what is now the northern United States. Mountains of ice would have blocked the migrating hunters' passage; no one knows how people passing over Beringia were able to reach the rest of the Americas.

Archaeologists have two main theories to explain how the early travelers managed to make their way south. One is called the Ice-Free Corridor theory. During the Ice Age, two main glaciers covered North America. The western glacier, the Cordilleran ice sheet, covered the area around the Rocky Mountains. The eastern glacier, the Laurentide ice sheet, covered all of eastern and central Canada, extending as far as the western plains. During the coldest times, when the ice was heaviest, these two ice sheets touched, and ice covered all of Canada from coast to coast. When the climate started to warm up a little, the ice began to shrink, leaving a narrow valley between the two ice sheets. In the 1950s, when scientists first arrived at the theory of the Ice-Free Corridor, archaeologists were excited, because they thought that migrating people must have traveled through this passageway as they followed the mammoth and antelope.

Scientists soon realized, however, that the Ice-Free Corridor theory had problems. For one thing, nobody had any evidence that such a migration took place. No signs of early humans have been found along the path of the corridor (although this lack of evidence does not rule out their presence, since any artifacts might have been destroyed over time). Scientists researching the theory paint a picture of what the corridor must have been like, a narrow channel lined with towering glaciers. The retreating ice would have left the corridor littered with broken rock and scraped free of soil. Few plants would have taken root at this early ice-free stage. Even the mammoths would not have wandered far into the corridor, giving humans even fewer reasons to travel south along it.

As the ice receded further and the corridor widened, the area between the two ice sheets may have become more inviting, encouraging animals and people to travel south through the continent. Mysteriously, however, archeological evidence indicates that southern settlements dated back to before the Ice-Free Corridor had widened to this point. If humans did not pass through the corridor, how did they reach these southern areas?

The other theory for humans' southern migration is that rather than traveling through the glaciers via the corridor, people went around the glaciers on foot or by boat. During the period of heaviest glaciation, the ice reached all the way to the ocean, leaving no land exposed for migrating people to travel on. As the ice began to pull back,

A South American Entry?

Although the prevailing theory is that the first people in the Americas came via the Bering Land Bridge, some scientists think early people may have arrived in South America by boat thousands of years before others migrated across Beringia. Stone tools found in South America appear to be at least 20,000 years old, older than any of the commonly accepted dates of North American sites.

Spear points are some of the earliest artifacts left behind by ancient human beings.

have visited are now all under water, submerged as the glaciers melted by the rising ocean levels. Any evidence of human passage would have been washed away thousands of years ago.

The earliest known evidence of humans in North America dates back at least 12,000 years. Some scientists have claimed to have found much earlier sites, but the dating of these settlements is still controversial and researchers have not generally agreed on them.

One of the oldest sites in Canada is Bluefish Caves in Yukon Territory. This site

the coastal land started to appear. People could have traveled this narrow strip of land between the Pacific Ocean and the glaciers. The travelers might also have journeyed along this route in skin boats, moving from island to island. The coastal lands these early people would

27

Some historians believe the earliest Americans went around the ice in boats.

exemplifies the dating controversy, since some scientists have dated it at 25,000 years old, but it is more commonly dated at 12,000 years old. A tool-marked mammoth bone and several stone tools were found in the caves, along with the bones of horse, bison, elk, and caribou.

Artifacts dating back around 12,000 years have also been found in the Queen Charlotte Islands, midway down the coast of British Columbia. These support the theory that some early people traveled down the Pacific Coast as they migrated south.

In the United States, south of the glacial

28

ice sheets, many more prehistoric sites have been found. One culture, called the Clovis people because archaeologists first found their artifacts near Clovis, New Mexico, lived on the plains from about 11,500 years ago until 11,000 years ago. For a long time, scientists thought the Clovis people were the oldest civilization in the United States, the first group to make their way south from the Bering Land Bridge. In the 1970s, though, archaeologists excavated a site in Meadowcroft, Pennsylvania, that apparently dates back almost 20,000 years. Not everyone agrees on this date, but since the discovery of Meadowcroft, more sites have been discovered across North and South America

Early North Americans lived in dwellings made from hide.

that also appear to date back at least this far. Deciphering the dates of the earliest North American settlements is a puzzle archaeologists are still studying and debating. When it comes to North America's long-ago settlement, the mystery of who, when, and how continues to fascinate historians and archeologists.

Studying the migration patterns and early settlements of the first inhabitants of North America is very challenging. Thousands of

What Does the Term "First Nations" Mean?

Many terms have been used to refer to the Native people of North America. In Canada, these people are usually called First Nations, because they literally lived in Canada first, thousands of years before Europeans or anyone else arrived. Other terms used to describe First Nations people include:

Indian—Christopher Columbus thought he had reached India when he landed in the Americas in 1492. For centuries people continued to call the Native North Americans Indians. Canada's official laws still refer to the First Nations as Indians.

Aboriginal People—Aboriginal means "existing from the beginning."

Native Canadians—This term was suggested to parallel the U.S. usage of Native Americans, but it never really caught on.

years have passed since these human beings' arrival. Glaciers have moved across the continent, raising and lowering ocean levels as the enormous sheets of ice melted and froze. Evidence from so long ago is extremely difficult to interpret. Many archaeological discoveries seem to make no sense. Bones and tools have shown that different groups of people had very different types of technologies, tools, and weapons. Human bones found with these tools show many groups also looked physically different from each other. Some were tall and slender, others shorter and sturdier. Some had broader faces and shorter skulls than others.

Whatever the truth about exactly how the first humans traveled through North America, settlement of these lands seems to have been a complex process, with different groups traveling along different routes and at different times. As archaeologists continue to uncover more information about the earliest North American settlers, our picture of events thousands of years ago may eventually become a little clearer. What we do know, however, is that once humans became established in the Americas, complex *cultures* and great civilizations arose. No written records tell us about life in these times; the first written accounts of life in the Americas would not be made until after Europeans came to these shores at the close of the fifteenth century. Nevertheless, long before Europeans arrived, the Americas were home to millions of people from thousands of cultural and language groups. Many of these people have been forever lost to history, but *archaeological* evidence and the First Nations groups that remain today can tell us much about those who lived in Canada before the Europeans' arrival.

*The shared beliefs and values of particular nations or groups make up their **cultures**.*

*Something that is **archaeological** relates to archaeology, the study of ancient cultures through the study of physical remains.*

Archaeologists have found a wide variety of ancient human bones in North America.

In the Mi'kmaq legend, a human form was created out of

Three

CANADA'S FIRST NATIONS: THE EAST

After Ootsitgamoo, the Earth, had been created and filled with plants and animals of every kind, Gisoolg decided to create Glooscap. Gisoolg caused a lightning bolt to hit Ootsitgamoo, and where the lightning had struck, a human form appeared out of the sand. Gisoolg threw another lightning bolt, and Glooscap became alive. But Glooscap could not move. He could only watch the birds and animals around him and Niskam the sun passing overhead in the sky. Glooscap asked Niskam for the freedom to move, and a third lightning bolt loosed him from the sand of Ootsitgamoo.

When Glooscap stood up, he turned around seven times. He looked up and gave thanks to Gisoolg for giving him life. He looked down at Ootsitgamoo and gave thanks for the sand that had created his body. He looked within himself and thanked Niskam for giving him his soul and spirit. Then Glooscap gave thanks to each of the four directions, East, North, West, and South. In this way he gave thanks to all seven directions.

The Mi'kmaq of Atlantic Canada tell this story of the creation of Glooscap, the first man, by Gisoolg, the Great Spirit. In some tales, Glooscap is a god. In others he is a man who has been given supernatural powers. In still others, Glooscap is simply the

Portage means to carry boats overland.

first man, who becomes a guide to his people. The Mi'kmaq are not the only group to tell the stories of Glooscap; the tale is shared by many other Algonquian nations.

The word Algonquian refers to a large number of First Nations groups who lived in northern Ontario and Quebec and in Atlantic Canada. The Algonquian groups spoke similar although not identical languages. Their lifestyles and traditions were also very much alike.

Algonquian Nations

Within the Algonquian language group, many individual tribal groups exist. Below are the names of some of the Algonquian nations that lived in northeastern Canada just before Europeans' fifteenth-century arrival.

Algonquin	Naskapi
Amalecite (Maliseet)	Ojibwa
Mi'kmaq	Ottawa
Montagnais	Tête de Boule

Many other nations speaking similar Algonquian dialects lived throughout the eastern half of what is now the United States. This connection of language groups suggests that many North American tribes are descended from the one group that migrated across the continent thousands of years ago.

Glooscap, the first man, was born from sand and lightning.

The Algonquian lived by hunting, trapping, and fishing, and by gathering berries and wild plants they found in the northern woods. The groups never stayed in one place for long, certainly not long enough to build permanent villages. Frequently, they traveled along waterways in birch bark canoes, which were lightweight and easy to build and also easy to carry when the people needed to *portage* around waterfalls or rapids.

During the summers, Algonquian tribal groups usually stayed together at fishing camps, living in wigwams. The bark-covered wigwams had round, dome-shaped frames. Generally, at least two families lived in one of these wigwams.

In the winter, the group split up into small family units. Each family would follow herds of deer or moose, hunting to survive during the long snowy months. The people stayed in smaller wigwams during the winter. These were conical rather than dome shaped and only large enough for one family.

Algonquian society was patrilineal, meaning the people traced their line of descent through the men of the group. Men led the tribes, and rights to hunting territories passed from father to son.

An artist's interpretation of the Algonquians' free-ranging life.

35

The Algonquian believed in a Great Spirit, usually called Gisoolg, who was neither male nor female. The word Gisoolg means "you have been created" and "the one created for your existence" in the Mi'kmaq language. Besides Gisoolg, the Algonquian believed in many less powerful spirits who inhabited nature. Evil spirits caused sickness and misfortune, while good spirits brought good fortune. Shamans, who communicated with the spirits, were an important part of tribal life.

Long ago, as the Iroquoian people tell it, the porcupine was chosen to lead the animals. One of the first things he did in his new position was call a council to decide whether it should remain night all the time or whether daylight should alternate with darkness. Some animals argued one way and some the other. The chipmunk wished for

the sun and for daylight. He began to sing, "The light must come! The light must come!" At the same time, the bear, who wanted darkness all the time, started to chant, "Night is best! Night is best!" Back and forth they went, but soon day began to dawn. The bear and his supporters were furious the chipmunk was winning. The bear leaped at the chipmunk to attack him, but the smaller animal darted into a hollow tree. The bear was able only to rake his claws along the chipmunk's back. To this day, the black marks of the bear's claws remain on the chipmunk's back. And ever since that time night and day have alternated.

While the Algonquian people roamed Canada's northern forests and eastern seacoasts,

The Algonquian traveled in birch-bark canoes.

the Iroquoian peoples lived in the fertile valleys and lowlands along the wide St. Lawrence River and the shores of the Great Lakes. Many people confuse the Iroquoian tribes with the Iroquois, a name that refers to an alliance of five (and later six) nations who lived in what is today New York State. The term Iroquoian, like Algonquian, actually refers to culturally similar people of a much larger language group. The Iroquoian group includes the Five Nations (Mohawk, Oneida, Onondaga, Cayuga, and Seneca), but also several nations who lived north of the Great Lakes in Canada.

*If something is **derogatory**, it is offensive and expresses a low opinion of something or someone.*

The largest of Canada's Iroquoian groups were the Wendat (today, the Wendat are commonly known by the name Huron, a name given to them by the French and viewed by many as *derogatory*) and the Neutrals. Although their languages and societies were similar, the Canadian Iroquoian fought numerous wars against the southern Five Nations Confederacy.

The Iroquoian lived in a very small area of land compared to the immense regions of the Algonquian, but their

A photograph of an Algonquian man taken in 1925 by Edward Curtis

Palisades are fences made of pointed stakes.

The Iroquoian relied on farming.

way of life allowed for denser populations and settlement. The Algonquian needed large areas over which to follow the animals they hunted. The Iroquoian, on the other hand, lived in settled communities that relied primarily on farming.

High wooden *palisades* surrounded Iroquoian villages to protect them from attacks by other tribes or by animals and to create a windbreak in the winter. Inside the palisade walls lay the longhouses. These structures were about twenty-three feet (7 meters) wide and ranged from forty-six feet (14 meters) long to over three hundred feet (over 91 meters). Large extended families lived in each longhouse, sometimes as many as fifty people in one building. Fields of corn, beans, and squash surrounded the outside of the village. The Iroquoian peoples called these crops the Three Sisters, the sustainers of life.

Since the Iroquoian societies lived more settled and structured lives than their Algonquian neighbors to their north,

The False Face Societies

Like the Algonquian, the Iroquoian believed in spirits and had shamans who communicated with the spirits for them. Members of the False Face Societies wore masks—false faces—the shaman had blessed and would visit the homes of the sick to drive out the evil spirits causing the sickness. Once a person had been cured by a False Face Society, that person could join the society and help cure others of the same sickness.

As many as fifty people lived in each longhouse.

the Iroquoian people developed complex cultural patterns. Their societies were matrilineal, tracing their familial lines through the women, and women held a great deal of power. The older women elected the village leaders. These leaders were men, but their positions rested on the favor of the women who had elected them. If the women saw fit, they could remove the male leaders from power. While the men hunted game or fought wars with neighboring nations, the women looked after the planting and harvesting of the crops.

Many people assume that when Europeans arrived in Canada, they stepped onto a largely unpopulated land. This is a serious misconception. Take, for example, popula-

tion estimates for the Wendat people. No one knows for sure how many Wendat lived in eastern Canada before the arrival of Europeans, but the lowest estimate is 25,000 (other estimates place the population at 40,000 or even more). How many longhouses might it take to shelter 25,000 people? If fifty people lived in each longhouse (most longhouses actually housed fewer than fifty people), at least five hundred longhouses would have clustered together in the Wendat's settlement area. And the Wendat were only one of the Iroquoian groups. If you think of all the people of the Iroquoian and the Algonquian groups, you can see that eastern Canada was actually a very well-populated region of the world.

But the eastern First Nations were not the only people who lived on the Canadian land before the Europeans' arrival. Other groups of people lived in the land to the west. On the plains and prairies, they developed unique cultures of their own, cultures that were shaped and nourished by the natural world where they lived.

According to the Iroquoian, the porcupine led the other animals as they decided whether daylight should alternate with darkness.

The Sun Dance held deep spiritual meaning for First Nations people.

Four
CANADA'S FIRST NATIONS: THE WEST

For three or four days, men danced inside the Sun Dance Lodge. Their dance was a sacred ritual that connected them to the spiritual world. Some of them were attached to the center pole of the lodge by skewers of wood or bone stuck through the skin of their chests. Other dancers fastened buffalo skulls to their backs. While the dance went on, the men did not eat or drink. Toward the end of the ceremony, many dancers began to see visions. Their dancing grew more frenzied, and they pulled against the skewers in their chests to rip them out of their skin. When all the dancers had broken free, the dance ended.

The sacred Sun Dance existed in many forms among the different people of the Plains. Today the most well-known version of the Sun Dance is the one in which dancers pierced their skin and were tethered to the center Sun Dance pole. Not all Plains People performed the ceremony in this way, but for those who did, the suffering of the dancers attached to the central pole was meant to ease the suffering of nature. Some stories tell of dancing to amuse the Sun so she will put an end to the hardships afflicting the people. The dancers' attachment to the center pole, which represents either the Earth or the sun, shows the connection between people and nature.

The First Nations of the Plains lived in tepees large enough for one family. The people traveled together in bands of about one hundred to two hundred people. These bands were not necessarily groups of relatives, and occasionally a band would divide, and its people would join other bands. The people of each band chose a leader based on his generosity, his prowess as a warrior, and

A Plains Indian

his ability to keep the people willing to accept his leadership.

Today, we often think of the People of the Plains as galloping across the open Prairies on horseback, but this picture did not become a reality until after the Spanish reintroduced the horse to North America in the 1500s. Thousands of years ago, horses had lived in North America, but they were hunted into extinction. In fact, the Plains Peoples of western Canada didn't acquire horses until the mid-1700s. (It took about two hundred years for trade routes to bring horses this far north.) Before the reintroduction of the horse, Plains Peoples used dogs to carry many of their belongings.

The First Nations of the Plains lived on the Prairies from the Great Lakes region to the Rocky Mountains. They had a vast territory, ranging south across the American plains and north to the beginnings of the dense forests in what is now the northern regions of the Prairie Provinces. Unlike the Algonquian and Iroquoian to the east, the Plains People did not all belong to a common language group. Instead, several different language groups lived on the Prairies.

The First Nations of the Plains (the Blackfoot, Plains Cree, Assinaboine, Sioux, and Crow were the largest groups) shared similar lifestyles and traditions, but their languages belonged to either the Algonquian,

The Plains People lived in tepees.

the Siouan, or the Athabascan language families. This difference in language is evidence that several separate groups had migrated into the area at different times, adapting to the culture of the region, which revolved around the buffalo herds.

Buffalo—or, more correctly, bison—were the center of life for the People of the Plains. Almost everything the people did was dependent on the buffalo and affected by the great animal's habits, movements, and populations. The Plains bands traveled across the Prairies following the herds. They ate buffalo meat and wore buffalo skins. Buffalo bones provided material for tools and weapons. Buffalo sinews gave them strong cords to be used as bowstrings or snares.

A bison, or North American buffalo

44

True buffalo, the wild oxen of India or Africa

Buffalo or Bison

Technically, buffalo are the wild oxen in India and in Africa. These animals are large, fierce, and very dangerous. Bison (also called the American buffalo) are a different animal native only to North America.

The Vision Quest

Most First Nations boys in their early teens went on a vision quest. The young man would go away by himself and fast, praying to the Great Spirit for guidance. He would then receive a vision from his spirit guide, who usually took the form of an animal. The tribal shaman would interpret the vision, which generally told the boy where to go to collect items to make up his medicine bundle. The medicine bundle consisted of sacred stones, feathers, or other objects. The things in a person's medicine bundle had special meaning to that person and represented his spiritual life.

A Native medicine wheel

Long ago, Raven was walking on the beach when he saw a large clamshell. Curious, he went over to it and looked inside. In the shell were tiny people. The people looked up at Raven with fear and wonder. Delighted, Raven coaxed the people to emerge. He was lonely, for the world was empty of all but a few animals in those days. Calmed by Raven's voice, the people stepped out of the shell. Before long, they had spread across the island, but they were helpless at first and did not know how to survive in this new world. Raven helped the people until they learned how to survive on the rocky Pacific island.

The tale of Raven's discovery of humankind in a clamshell is told in various forms by many of the people of the Pacific Northwest, such as the Haida of the Queen Charlotte Islands and the Tlingit and Tsimshian of coastal British Columbia. Raven is the most important figure in the stories of these cultures. Though he is the caretaker of humans, he is also a trickster who loves to play jokes on people.

The cultures of the Pacific Northwest peoples were the most complex of all Canadian First Nations societies. In the time before Europeans arrived in North America, the area was more densely populated than the rest of Canada and included a great

Ravens of the Northwest

number of very different language groups. The First Nations of the Pacific Northwest spoke at least nineteen completely distinct language types.

Despite these language differences, the cultures of the Pacific Northwest people were remarkably similar. Rows of cedar-plank houses made up the villages, with the

47

People of the Northwest

chief living in the largest house at the village center. The upper-class nobles had the best houses with plank roofs, while the poorer people had to make do with bark roofs. The richer village members also kept slaves captured from other tribes during wars or raids. Slaves had no rights at all. Poor commoners had some rights, but they needed to buy many of them. Commoners had to pay for hunting rights and to come to the gathering places near the village.

The diet of the Pacific Northwest peoples consisted of salmon and other fish, seals, whales, deer, elk, bears, mountain goats, berries, and various plants. The sea and land overflowed with food for these early First Nations.

Totem poles portrayed the Northwest First Nations' vision of the spiritual world.

Like most Canadian First Nations people the people of the Pacific Northwest believed in a Great Spirit and in many lesser spirits. Shamans talked to the spirits on behalf of the people, and people consulted the shamans for help with sicknesses, births, hunting expeditions, and problems with weather or nature. Shamans needed to communicate with evil spirits as well as good spirits, and because of this they lived by themselves outside of the villages.

The greatest festival of the Pacific Northwest people was the Potlatch celebration. Potlatches celebrated marriages, births, the selection of a new chief, or the raising of a new totem pole, carved to tell the stories of

A Potlatch gathering

49

A First Nations' shelter in the Canadian Northwest

clans or events. At a Potlatch, the chief of one village would invite chiefs and guests from neighboring villages to come enjoy his generosity. The Potlatch was a giving celebration; guests were heaped with gifts of all sorts—blankets, artwork, jewelry, hunting rights to certain lands, canoes—and they feasted on more food than anyone could ever eat. Later, the guests would respond by throwing their own Potlatch and by trying to outdo their host in generosity. Potlatches helped to redistribute the wealth of the clans and made sure no one became too attached to material riches. In some tribes, Potlatches eventually became a way to ruin a rival chief by forcing him to throw a lavish Potlatch he could not afford. This was not the case in most areas of the Pacific Northwest, however.

The culture of the First Nations of the Plains grew out of the wide flatland on which they lived and from their dependence on the migrating buffalo herds. The First Nations of the Pacific Northwest, on the other hand, lived in a lush land of abundant resources and this bounty shaped their settled, complex society. Meanwhile, the people to the north lived in a different environment all together.

People of the Interior

Between the western Coast Mountains and the Rocky Mountains, in the high valleys, lived several groups of First Nations people who were neither exactly like the People of the Plains or those of the Pacific Northwest. Some of these tribes, such as the Kutenai, came from the east and had once been part of the First Nations of the Plains. Others, like the Interior Salish, had come inland from the west, where they had once lived with the Coast Salish along the Pacific Ocean. Each group kept parts of the cultures from which they came, but each had to adapt to life between the mountain ranges.

Five

CANADA'S FIRST NATIONS: THE NORTH

At one time, winter kept the land in its cold grasp all year round. Everything was frozen; the lakes and rivers stayed solid and icy. No plants could grow in the snow and cold. One day, when the Dene were out hunting, they met a bear with a bag tied around his neck.

"What is in the bag?" the hunters asked.

"Summer is in this bag," answered the bear, "with all its light and warmth."

Then the Dene hunters tried to convince the bear to trade for the bag, but the bear refused.

When the hunters returned home, they told their chief about the bear and his bag of summer. The chief wanted the bag too, and together they came up with a plan to get it.

"We will invite the bear to a feast," said the chief. "After he eats, he will fall asleep, and then we will take the bag."

The Athabascan hunted moose and caribou, and caught salmon from the streams.

So the hunters went out to search for the bear and invite him to a feast. Then they prepared a banquet of moose and caribou and sat back awaiting the bear's arrival. But when the bear appeared, he was not wearing the bag. The Dene were terribly disappointed, but they served the bear the feast anyway, and afterward he fell asleep. While he was asleep, the chief gathered four of his best hunters and told them to follow the bear home after he awoke.

For an hour, the hunters followed the bear through the snow, until at last they came to a cave. Looking inside, the hunters saw the bag lying on the floor guarded by two other bears. The hunters leaped inside the cave to take the bag. In the fight that followed, three of the hunters were killed and the fourth badly wounded. Just before he died, the fourth hunter grabbed the bag and pulled it open.

Immediately, the sky was lit with sunshine, and warmth flooded over the land. The rivers and lakes thawed and flowers bloomed across the hillsides. Birds fluttered singing into the air. Ever since that time, the Dene have had both summer and winter seasons.

In the north of Canada live the Athabascans, among them the Dene and the Chipewyan. The Athabascans are a language group, closely related to the languages of the Navajo and Apache in the American Southwest. The Canadian Athabascan lived in the Northwest Territories, Yukon Territory, and in northern Manitoba, Saskatchewan, Alberta, and British Columbia.

Culturally, the Athabascans were very similar to the eastern Algonquian people. They were nomadic, following the migrations of the animals they hunted. Some tribes mainly hunted caribou; others hunted moose or mountain sheep. Many fished for salmon in the rivers, coming together during the summer in fishing camps like the Algonquian people did. Also, like the Algonquians, the Athabascans tended to divide into smaller groups for the winter, with each family providing for its own needs during the winter months.

Some Athabascans built domed houses covered with bark or skins; others built shelters of poles and sod. The construction of these lodgings varied among tribes. Usually,

Many Athabascans fished for salmon in the rivers.

Caribou

their shelters had to be easy to build and transport and quick to set up. During the winters, the people traveled long distances on foot through the snow, following the migrations of the caribou or moose.

Since the Athabascans rarely lived together in large groups, they did not need to appoint tribal chiefs. The oldest female family member led the clan, guiding the family through important decisions.

One night, all the Inuit were at a drum dance, a celebration often performed when everyone came together. One girl did not want to go to the dance, so she went to an igloo by herself. Suddenly, someone ran in,

Animal Spirits

Most First Nations peoples believed in spirits, both good and evil. Many believed each person had a guardian spirit who often appeared in the shape of a certain animal. Some animals also had meaning to different cultures, like Raven in the nations of the Pacific Northwest. The Athabascans believed the crow and owl spoke to people. To help them in their rituals and their communication with the spirits, shamans sometimes used "spirit-helpers" carved of ivory in the shape of animals.

blew out the lamp, and pulled her hair. By the time she had lit the lamp again, the person was nowhere to be seen. Wanting to find out who had done this, the girl put ashes in her hair and waited to see if the person would come again.

Inuit carving of igloos

57

Sure enough, soon the same thing happened all over again. The girl slipped out of the igloo and went over to where all the people had gathered. She looked at the people to see who had ashes smeared on their hands. She saw that her brother had dirty hands and was laughing at her from beside the group of dancers.

Angrily, she grabbed a torch and ran after him. He grabbed another torch and ran away, but he slipped and fell as he ran. The torch almost went out; only a little glow remained. The boy ran on with his sister chasing him, and slowly they began to rise up from the land. The girl became the sun and the boy the moon, and now they chase each other across the sky.

The Inuit of the Far North were the last of the First Nations to arrive in Canada, coming four thousand to five thousand years ago. In the past, the Inuit have been called Eskimos, an Algonquian word meaning "eaters of raw meat." The Inuit themselves never use the term Eskimo and consider it an insult. In their language, the word Inuit means "the people." Some groups within the region have their own names for themselves, such as the Inuvialuit, which means "real human beings," in the western parts of the Canadian Arctic.

The Inuit people lived across the North

The First Nations of the far north called themselves Inuit, "the people."

American Arctic, north of the tree line. Since the climate is so extreme in the Far North, the Inuit had to be very creative to survive. They hunted caribou and seals, as well as walruses, sea lions, and whales, and they used almost every part of the animals. Sealskin made waterproof boots. Caribou skins made warm winter parkas. Seal oil could be burned in lamps. Igloos made of ice blocks served as shelters.

The Inuit made kayaks using whalebone or driftwood frames covered with skins. The hunter sat in a hole in the center of the kayak so the skins covering the boat encircled his waist. He then attached his parka to the opening, which kept the water out. If a kayak happened to turn over, hunters knew the trick of quickly rolling it upright. Since they were sealed in, no water got into the kayak. Larger skin-covered boats called *umiak* carried families and belongings.

The Inuit had no real tribal organization, although the people within a region would gather during the winter in sealing camps. Often these groups included many related families. Each family was led by its oldest hunter, and the oldest hunter within a larger group unofficially took charge.

To transport their belongings in the winter, the Inuit used sleds pulled by sled dogs. The sleds, called *komatiks*, ranged in length from about ten to twenty feet (3 to 6 meters).

Komatiks could carry people as well, but often the Inuit walked, wearing snowshoes to stay on top of the snow. To make the komatiks go faster, the Inuit poured water onto the sled runners to make ice.

One of the most important figures in Inuit religion is the sea goddess Sedna, who was once human. She married a bird who could transform into a man. Sedna's husband, however, mistreated her, so her father came and killed him. As Sedna's father returned home with his daughter, many birds, angry

Sedna's fingers turned into walruses.

*To **appease** means to do whatever it takes to keep someone from being upset or angry.*

at the death of their friend, came and attacked the boat. Frightened, Sedna's father took hold of his daughter and threw her over the side of the boat to **appease** the birds. But Sedna grabbed the side of the boat as she fell and would not let go. Her father became desperate; he took out his knife and cut Sedna's fingers off so she would let go. Sedna fell into the sea, and her fingers became whales, seals, and walruses. Sedna, however, did not die. She became the goddess of the sea. The top of her body stayed that of a woman, but the bottom half became the tail of a fish.

The Inuit believe Sedna has control over all the creatures of the sea. Sometimes, when the hunters begin to have trouble finding sea animals, they send a shaman to visit Sedna. The shaman must change himself into a fish and swim down to the bottom of the sea where Sedna lives. There, he

An Inuit puppy that will grow up to be a sled dog

combs and braids her hair, which makes her happy. Then the sea animals become plentiful again.

Like the other First Nations, the Inuit and the other people of the North had deep spiritual beliefs. The Earth and the natural world shaped their concept of life's deepest meaning. When the Europeans arrived in their land, First Nations peoples would encounter new spiritual concepts as well as an entire new way of life.

The natural world shaped the Inuit's concept of the spiritual realm.

61

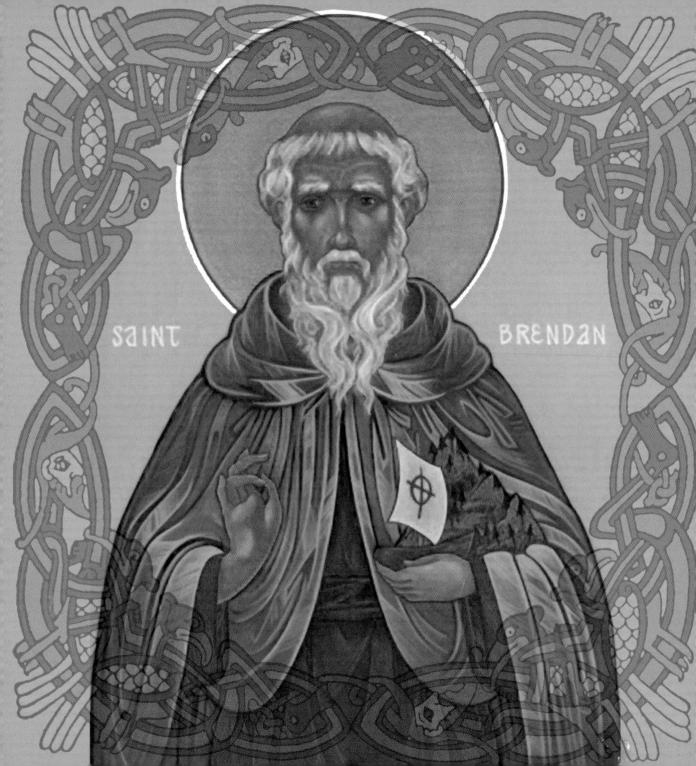

Six
EARLY VISITORS TO CANADA

"If it be only God's holy will, I have in my heart resolved to go forth in quest of the Land of Promise of the Saints," St. Brendan said to the monks with him.

All the monks agreed, and they set out, leaving Ireland in their little cowhide *curragh*. Seven years later, after voyaging to many islands and seeing many wonders, they came to another shore and "when they had disembarked, they saw a land, extensive and thickly set with trees, laden with fruits, as in the autumn season." The monks explored this new land for many days, but they could not find the end of it. At last they met a young man who told them this was the land St. Brendan had been seeking. Until this time, the man said, God had hidden the land from sight, but in the future, when a time of persecution came on the Church, the land would be open to the people of God.

*A **curragh** is a small boat with a wicker frame.*

*A **monastery** is a place where monks live together.*

When Europeans first came to North America is not definitely known, but some believe that St. Brendan may have been the first to set foot on this continent. St. Brendan, who lived in Ireland in the sixth century, was an abbot, a monk in charge of all the monks in a **monastery**. The document *The Voyage of St. Brendan the Abbot* tells of his long journey to the "Land Promised to the Saints." Some believe this journey may have taken St. Brendan all the way to the shores of Newfoundland. The document, however, was written three hundred years after St. Brendan lived, which is one of the reasons people are skeptical about the truth of the story.

For many years, scientists thought an extended journey across the North Atlantic in a tiny skin boat would have been impossible. In 1976 and 1977, however, historian Tim Severin set out to prove the voyage could be made. He successfully re-created the expedition in a boat like the one described in

Early map of Ireland

St. Brendan

St. Brendan's crystal column may have been an iceberg.

The Voyage of St. Brendan the Abbot. Severin's experiment did not prove St. Brendan actually traveled to North America, of course, but it did show that such a journey was at least possible.

The Irish had a reputation for being good sailors, and Irish monks did travel to many of the islands around the British Isles, founding monasteries there. Clues within the manuscript itself lead historians to believe St. Brendan—or someone else—journeyed far into the North Atlantic. Islands described in *The Voyage of St. Brendan the*

Abbot seem to include the Shetland Islands, the Faeroe Islands, and Iceland. A column of crystal mentioned in the text could easily be an iceberg, and a large sea creature spouting foam from its head sounds something like a whale.

Whether St. Brendan and his monks actually made it as far as Newfoundland is uncertain. In the narrative, when the monks reach the Land Promised to the Saints, the story becomes even stranger than it was at first. Wonderful fruits grow on every tree, and precious stones are everywhere. A beautiful young man greets the travelers with a message from God. After reading the account of the voyage, scholar Geoffrey Ashe concluded that the first part of *The Voyage of St. Brendan the Abbot* described a real expedition, but that the section describing the Land Promised to the Saints referred to a vision of a promised world to come.

No archaeological evidence exists to suggest Irish monks reached the east coast of Canada in the mid-500s CE. Still, there is a possibility that the story is true. St. Brendan could have traveled north in a curragh from Ireland to Iceland and then west and south to Greenland and then to Newfoundland. Tim Severin proved it was possible and no evidence exists to disprove the story.

After they left the forested coasts of Markland, Leif Eriksson and the other Vikings sailed for another two days until they reached a new land. To its north was an island, and here they put ashore. Dew covered the grass, and the men gathered it up in their hands and drank it. Nothing had ever tasted sweeter.

Irish monks may or may not have made a trek to Canadian shores. Most scholars agree, however, that the Vikings did. Around 1000 CE, these seafaring warriors from Scandinavia were near the height of their power. For over one hundred years they had explored and raided the coasts of Europe and would continue their attacks until most of them converted to Christianity in the 1100s. In the late 800s, the Vikings colonized Iceland. Some Vikings then chose to travel southwest around the coast of Europe. Others slowly began to set out into the unknown west of Iceland. Some scholars speculate that the Vikings might have heard of western lands from the Irish, who knew of them from the voyages of St. Brendan.

In 1000, Leif Eriksson sailed away from the Viking colony that his father, Erik the Red, had founded in Greenland fifteen years before. He came first to a land of flat rock that he named Helluland (stone-slab land). This was probably Baffin Island in Canada's Nunavut Territory. He then came to a land he named Markland (forest land). Two days out of Markland, Leif Eriksson came to what he named Vinland. Vinland was a pleasant place, and the Vikings put ashore and built houses, founding a short-lived colony. The Vikings later recorded the story of Leif Eriksson's journey and the discovery of Vinland.

The location of Vinland has never been completely determined. Some people think it was in Ungava Bay in northern Quebec. Others believe it was in Nova Scotia, New Brunswick, or even as far south as New

England. Many are convinced the Viking settlement of Vinland was located in L'Anse aux Meadows, at the tip of the Great Northern Peninsula in Newfoundland.

We may never know for sure whether or not L'Anse aux Meadows was the Vinland described in the Viking sagas, but we do know the Vikings were there around the same time as the discovery of Vinland. In the 1960s, archaeologists Helge and Anne Stine Ingstad led a series of excavations in L'Anse aux Meadows, uncovering the remains of three large sod houses and a number of smaller buildings. The Ingstads and other archaeologists in later Parks Canada excavations found many Norse artifacts, including stone lamps, bronze cloak pins, and boat nails at the site.

The Newfoundland coast, where Vikings may have landed in 1000 CE

Dating Systems and Their Meaning

You might be accustomed to seeing dates expressed with the abbreviations BC or AD, as in the year 1000 BC or the year AD 1900. For centuries, this dating system has been the most common in the Western world. However, since BC and AD are based on Christianity (BC stands for Before Christ and AD stands for anno Domini, Latin for "in the year of our Lord"), many people now prefer to use abbreviations that people from all religions can be comfortable using. The abbreviations BCE (meaning Before Common Era) and CE (meaning Common Era) mark time in the same way (for example, 1000 BC is the same year as 1000 BCE, and AD 1900 is the same year as 1900 CE), but BCE and CE do not have the same religious overtones as BC and AD.

The archaeological evidence found in L'Anse aux Meadows is the only generally accepted proof of a European presence in North America before its official "discovery" in 1492 by Christopher Columbus.

Another interesting but very controversial theory says that Earl Henry Sinclair, a Scottish nobleman, journeyed to Nova Scotia in 1398. According to the theory, Sinclair traveled across the North Atlantic with Nicolo and Antonio Zeno, seafarers from an important family in Venice, Italy. Another part of the theory says Sinclair either founded or influenced the Mi'kmaq tribe of Nova Scotia, becoming, in fact, their mythical figure Glooscap.

The idea began with the 1558 publication of a book in Venice by Nicolo Zeno that claimed his ancestors, Nicolo and Antonio Zeno, had voyaged across the North Atlantic with a Prince Zichmni who came from somewhere north of Britain. The book was apparently based on letters written by the Zeno brothers and a map drawn by them showing the islands of the North Atlantic. Many scholars today think the sixteenth-century Zeno invented the letters and map.

Believing the theory requires believing first that Zeno did not make up the letters and map; second, that if the letters described a real voyage, the expedition actually did go to Nova Scotia; and third, that Prince Zichmni actually was Henry Sinclair, earl of the Orkney Islands. Those who do believe Sinclair reached North America accept these difficulties easily and claim to have other proof as well. Writer Frederick Pohl draws many parallels between the Mi'kmaq legends of Glooscap and Henry Sinclair. In some versions of the legends, Glooscap arrives from the east in a great stone canoe, bringing wisdom and aid to the people of Nova Scotia. Pohl believes the name Glooscap is the Mi'kmaq pronunciation of Jarl (Earl) Sinclair. Others have drawn attention to similarities between the Mi'kmaq flag and the flag of the *Knights Templar*, of which Sinclair was said to be a member.

Very few historians, however, believe Sinclair traveled to North America. No convincing archaeological proof exists, and the fact that the theory did not exist until centuries after Sinclair's death also makes the idea very unlikely.

Tales about voyages to distant, fantastic lands have existed for thousands of years. Almost every culture seems to have its own story about an explorer who discovered a new land—now almost always identified as North America. In 330 BCE, the Greek mathematician and explorer Pytheas wrote about a voyage to the land of Thule, beyond Great Britain to the north. Some believe Welsh Prince Madoc came to North America in 1170 CE and founded a colony, intermarrying with the Native people. The Basque, the Portuguese, and the English all have claimed at various times to have arrived first, before Columbus officially discovered the New World.

In truth, we have little evidence that anyone, other than the Vikings, walked the shores of Canada before the late 1400s. But in the fifteenth century, all that would change.

*The **Knights Templar** is a fraternal group originally formed to protect Christians traveling to Jerusalem, and now a part of the Free and Accepted Masons.*

Was L'Anse aux Meadows Vinland?

Scientists and historians have evidence arguing both for and against the idea that L'Anse aux Meadows, Newfoundland, was the Viking Vinland. On one hand, the description of Vinland in the Viking sagas tells of the discovery of wild grapes, and the name Vinland seems to mean wine land. Grapes have never grown as far north as L'Anse aux Meadows. Butternuts have been found at L'Anse aux Meadows, however, and these too have never grown so far north. This suggests the Vikings did travel further south and brought the butternuts back to L'Anse aux Meadows.

On the other hand, the description of wild grapes might refer to any of the many types of berries growing wild in northern Newfoundland, and wine could be made from these berries as well as from grapes. Also, no other locations were named in the sagas to account for the L'Anse aux Meadows site, which was occupied for several years by nearly a hundred people.

A European map of the world from the 1500s

Seven

FIRST CONTACT: EUROPEAN EXPLORERS ARRIVE

Even though the Vikings (and perhaps a few other Europeans) had reached Canadian shores, their brief stays appear to have had little to no impact on the First Nations peoples living throughout North America. In the late 1400s, however, the true "first contact" with Europeans occurred, changing the First Nations' lives forever.

European nations had been making overland trade expeditions to the *Far East* for many years when, in the 1400s, a *blockade* by the growing *Muslim* empire forced them to look for alternate routes. Some traders chose to sail around Africa, but this was a long, difficult journey. Christopher Columbus decided it would be quicker and easier to simply sail west across the ocean, which he calculated would bring him around the world and to the eastern shores of Asia. Any expeditions that may have been made (by the Vikings or by others) hundreds of years before had been lost to history, and Europeans had no idea that a vast land lay to their west.

When Columbus, traveling on behalf of Spain, landed in the Bahamas in 1492, he believed he had discovered what he was looking for: a sea route to India and Southeast Asia. His

The Far East is a term that was historically used to describe the countries of eastern Asia.

A blockade is an organized act to prevent goods or people from leaving or entering a place.

A Muslim is someone who follows the beliefs and practices of the religion of Islam.

Christopher Columbus

the ship moved out of the harbor and unfurled England's red cross flying from the top of the mast. Europe's discovery of Canada was about to begin.

Cabot, of course, was not trying to discover Canada. He wanted, like Columbus, to discover a trade route to the Far East. He was an Italian sailor (originally named

John Cabot

discovery left other European nations eager to establish their own Atlantic trade routes with the East.

In May 1497, John Cabot and a crew of eighteen set sail from Bristol, England, in the little ship the *Matthew*. Cabot carried letters granting him rights of exploration and discovery on behalf of England's King Henry VII. Wind caught the white sails as

Henry VII of England

73

The title page from a 1607 account of the Corte-Reals' voyage

Giovanni Caboto) and a friend of Christopher Columbus. He had not been able to gain support for his expedition from either Spain or Portugal, so he went to England. He found the backing he needed both from Henry VII and from the Bristol merchants who helped fund his expedition.

The journey took just over a month, and Cabot made landfall on June 24, 1497. The exact location of Cabot's first landing in North America is controversial. He may have landed in Newfoundland, Nova Scotia, or possibly even Maine.

Cabot explored the coast for about a month and then returned to England. The next year, King Henry sent Cabot out again, this time with more ships and instructions to explore further. Nothing was ever heard from Cabot again. He and his ships could have gone down in a storm, or the party could have been attacked and lost in North America.

Cabot is famous not so much for what he did as for what he started. He was the first European to officially set foot in North America, the first proven European since the Vikings nearly five hundred years before him. With Cabot's discovery, Europe began to realize they had found not the trade route they were seeking but an entirely unknown land.

Sixteenth-century map of the cod fishing in Newfoundland and Labrador

Even though Europeans had begun to realize North America was not, in fact, the Asian land they sought, they thought it was probably a fairly narrow land. All they needed to do, they decided, was find a river cutting through the new land. Then they could sail their ships along the river, come out in the Pacific Ocean, and continue sailing toward Asia. They called this fabled route the Northwest Passage, and for centuries explorers would travel along every North American river in an effort to find it.

In 1500, King Manuel I of Portugal sent Gaspar and Miguel Corte-Real to find a route through the newly discovered country. The Corte-Reals sailed around Newfoundland and along the coast of Labrador, but found no satisfying rivers leading inland to the west. The expedition was not a huge success; eventually both brothers were lost at sea in the waters near Newfoundland.

The deaths of the Corte-Reals did not deter Portugal from their explorations of the "New World." In 1521, João Alvares Fagundes sailed west along the south coast of Newfoundland and possibly into the Gulf of St. Lawrence. Little is known about Fagundes' voyage, but some people believe he tried to found a Portuguese colony on Cape Breton Island in Nova Scotia. Almost nothing is known about this possible colony, and no evidence of it has ever been found. According to the theory, however, the colony did not last long and was abandoned after troubles with the Natives in the area.

Portugal's exploration of Canada was short-lived, although they did continue sending fishing ships to the Grand Banks off Newfoundland's coast. A handful of place

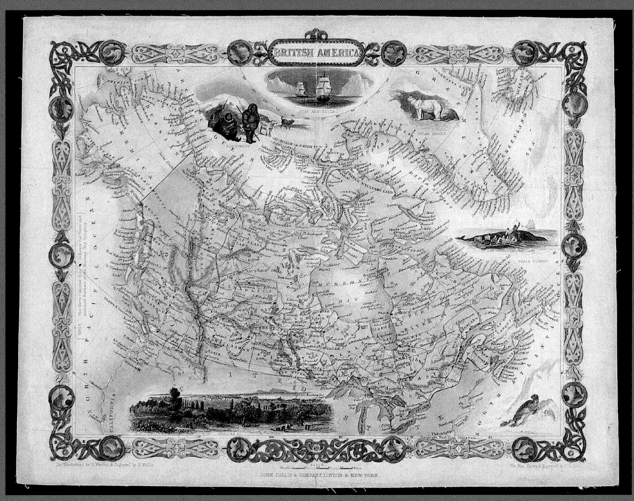

An early British map of Canada

names in Atlantic Canada—such as the Bay of Fundy and Labrador (from lavrador meaning "landowner")—survive as a legacy of Portugal's early North American presence.

During the first few decades of the sixteenth century, most of the seafaring European nations sent ships to the Canadian coast, although most of them did not establish permanent settlements. Many came to fish in the cod-rich Grand Banks. The *Basque* came for the fish and discovered the whales. Soon, the nations of Europe would begin to turn their thoughts to colonizing the New World, with its riches of fish, timber, and other natural resources, and then the race to claim the land would begin in earnest. Canada, for thousands of years inhabited by hundreds of First Nations tribes, had been discovered by the rest of the world.

*The **Basque** are people of unknown origin living in the western Pyrenees, in northeastern Spain, and southwestern France.*

The Naming of America

In 1507, on a map created by German cartographer Martin Waldseemüller, the name America appeared for the first time, written across the newly discovered land to the west. Waldseemüller named the new land after the Latin form of the name of Portuguese explorer, Amerigo Vespucci. America appears on the map as a long thin sliver of land. Along the eastern coast, the newly named places are labeled neatly, while the nearby western coast is left bare, as yet unexplored.

1170 Welsh Prince Madoc believed by some to found colony in North America.

500–1000 According to some, the voyage of St. Brendan the Abbot from Ireland to Newfoundland occurs sometime between these dates.

1492 Christopher Columbus arrives in the Americas.

1398 Scottish nobleman Earl Henry Sinclair is believed by some to arrive in Novia Scotia.

1000 Viking Leif Eriksson arrives at Helluland (believed by many to be Baffin Island).

1500s The Spanish reintroduce the horse to North America.

1507 The name America appears on a map for the first time.

June 24, 1497 Italian John Cabot makes landfall in North America.

1500 Gaspar and Miguel Corte-Real of Portugal sail around Newfoundland and along the coast of Labrador.

1521 João Alvares Fagundes of Portugal sails along the southern coast of Newfoundland and possibly into the Gulf of St. Lawrence.

mid-1700s The Plains People of western Canada acquire horses.

1936 Human artifacts found in a cave near Clovis, New Mexico.

late 1800s Vikings colonize Iceland.

80

1960s Helge and Anne Stine Ingstad unearth Norse artifacts in L'Anse aux Meadows.

1973–1977 James Adovasio excavates the area at Meadowcroft, Pennsylvania.

1950s Scientists derive the Ice-Free Corridor theory.

1976 Historian Tim Severin re-creates the voyage of St. Brendan the Abbot.

81

FURTHER READING

Bial, Raymond. *The Haida.* New York: Benchmark Books, 2001.

Bonvillain, Nancy. *The Inuit.* New York: Chelsea House, 1995.

Fitzhugh, William W., and Elisabeth I. Ward, eds. *Vikings: The North Atlantic Saga.* Washington, D.C.: Smithsonian Institution Press, 2000.

Lauber, Patricia. *Who Came First? New Clues to Prehistoric Americans.* Washington, D.C.: National Geographic, 2003.

Leon, George DeLucenay. *Explorers of the Americas Before Columbus.* New York: Franklin Watts, 1989.

Libal, Autumn. *North American Indians Today: Huron.* Philadelphia, Pa.: Mason Crest Publishers, 2004.

Rengel, Marian. *John Cabot: The Ongoing Search for a Westward Passage to Asia.* New York: Rosen Publishing Group, 2003.

Rogers, Barbara Radcliffe, and Stillman D. Rogers. *Canada: Enchantment of the World.* New York: Children's Press, 2000.

Sattler, Helen Roney. *The Earliest Americans.* New York: Clarion Books, 1993.

Thompson, Linda. *People of the Plains and Prairies.* Vero Beach, Fla.: Rourke Publishing, 2003.

FOR MORE INFORMATION

Algonquin.tv
www.algonquin.tv

L'Anse Aux Meadows National
Historic Site
www.pc.gc.ca/lhn-nhs/nl/meadows/
natcul/hist_e.asp

The Atlas of Canada
atlas.gc.ca

Canada's First Nations Project
www.ucalgary.ca/applied_history/tutor/
firstnations/home

Canadian Biodiversity Website
www.canadianbiodiversity.mcgill.ca

Canadian Museum of Civilization
www.civilization.ca

Luxton Museum of the Plains Indian
collections.ic.gc.ca/luxton

Native Peoples of Canada
collections.ic.gc.ca/nativepeoples

Newfoundland and Labrador Heritage:
Exploration and Settlement
www.heritage.nf.ca/exploration

Virtual Museum of Canada:
Haida and Inuit Exhibition
www.virtualmuseum.ca/Exhibitions/
Inuit_Haida/English

Publisher's note:
The Web sites listed on this page were active at the time of publication. The publisher is not responsible for Web sites that have changed their addresses or discontinued operation since the date of publication. The publisher will review and update the Web-site list upon each reprint.

INDEX

PICTURE CREDITS

Benjamin Stewart: pp. 10, 19, 24 bottom left, 24 bottom right, 56, 58, 59, 60, 60–61

Community of St. Columcille: p. 62

Corel: pp. 1, 16, 22–23

Edward S. Curtis, Library of Congress: pp. 28, 36–37, 37 bottom right, 42, 43

Government of Ontario, Edward Morris: p. 35 bottom right

Hemera Images: pp. 8–9, 11, 12, 15, 16–17, 18, 26–27, 29, 30–31, 35 top left, 38–39, 52, 54, 55, 57, 65, 78–79, 80–81

Intuitive Media: pp. 32–33

Library of Congress: p. 49

Memorial University of Newfoundland: p. 64 bottom right

National Archives of Canada: pp. 70–71, 72 left

National Library of Canada: pp. 24 top left, 38, 74, 75, 76

Photos.com: pp. 21, 44, 45, 47, 49 right, 50

Sharon Stewart: pp. 66–69

University of Wisconsin: pp. 40–41

To the best knowledge of the publisher, all other images are in the public domain. If any image has been inadvertently uncredited, please notify Harding House Publishing Service, Vestal, New York 13850, so that rectification can be made for future printings.

BIOGRAPHIES

Sheila Nelson was born in Newfoundland and grew up very near the Viking site in L'Anse aux Meadows. She has written a number of history books for kids and always enjoys the chance to keep learning. She recently earned a master's degree and now lives in Rochester, New York, with her husband and daughter.

SERIES CONSULTANT

Dr. David Bercuson is the Director of the Centre for Military and Strategic Studies at the University of Calgary. His writings on modern Canadian politics, Canadian defense and foreign policy, and Canadian military, among other topics, have appeared in academic and popular publications. Dr. Bercuson is the author, coauthor, or editor of more than thirty books, including *Confrontation at Winnipeg: Labour, Industrial Relations, and the General Strike* (1990), *Colonies: Canada to 1867* (1992), *Maple Leaf Against the Axis, Canada's Second World War* (1995), and *Christmas in Washington: Roosevelt and Churchill Forge the Alliance* (2005). He has also served as historical consultant for several film and television projects, and provided political commentary for CBC radio and television and CTV television. In 1989, Dr. Bercuson was elected a fellow of the Royal Society of Canada. In 2004, Dr. Bercuson received the Vimy Award, sponsored by the Conference of Defence Association Institute, in recognition of his significant contributions to Canada's defense and the preservation of the Canadian democratic principles.